THE GUARDIAN

Gil McDonald

The Guardian
Copyright© 2016 Gil McDonald-Constable
Cover Design Livia Reasoner
Fire Star Press
www.firestarpress.com

All rights reserved.
ISBN-13: 978-1537788814
ISBN-10: 1537788817

This is a work of fiction. The characters, incidents, and dialogues are products of the author's imagination and are not to be construed as real.

No part of this book may be used or reproduced in any manner whatsoever without written permission of the publisher, except in the case of brief quotations embodied in critical articles and reviews.

DEDICATION

To the Ladies who provided the prompts. Thank you.

THE GUARDIAN

CHAPTER ONE

He was there again. Bill Crowley. Sitting at the corner table next to the window, gazing out on the world, trilby on the table, mug of tea clutched in both hands in a 'don't even speak to me' attitude.

Maybe I shouldn't have, but of course I spoke to him, always did. Been doing it for months now, don't know why, because he's rarely said much back to me, but something drew me to him from the first day I saw him there. Maybe it was just because he looked lonely, and I've never liked the idea of an elderly person being lonely. What is it they say? "There but for the grace," and all that? One day, it could be me.

I paid for my breakfast and headed for his table. He didn't even look up as I parked myself on the chair and doused my fry up in dollops of thick tomato sauce.

"Alright, Bill?"

I speared a big forkful of sausage and egg and shoved it in

my mouth as I waited for him to acknowledge me.

I didn't know much about him; we'd spoken before, of course, but it was usually in monosyllables. I know he looked a lot like my granddad, thin grey hair, slim, with an almost military bearing, spoiled somewhat by that hunched-up appearance elderly folk often have. His watery blue eyes had a far-away look behind round, wire-framed glasses. I reckon that was why I'd taken to sitting at his table actually, my old gramps had left this world a couple of years back, and I missed him. He'd been my last living relative. I guess Bill Crowley was a sort of surrogate.

He grunted a greeting and carried on staring over my shoulder out of the window, as if he was seeing a different place—not this cold, miserable town—but somewhere he'd been happy once, maybe.

"Want some fried bread?" I beckoned toward my heaped plate.

He shook his head. Today was going to be a quiet one. He had his days. Sometimes he'd talk, other times, like now, he'd say hardly anything. Oh, well. I didn't mind. I'd be on my way as soon as I'd finished eating, anyway. Busy day at work. I speared another mushroom.

"I'm tired now."

His voice was so quiet I wasn't sure he'd actually spoken. I stopped chewing so I could hear him a bit better.

"Sorry, what did you say?"

"Tired. I'm getting tired. Seen too much, now. Time to be off, I think."

That worried me. What was he talking about? If he was thinking of topping himself, I should really try to talk him out of it…shouldn't I?

"You okay, mate? If you need to talk, I'm free for a while. What's bothering you?"

Well, I *could* be free. I mean, I'd never forgive myself if the old guy topped himself just because I didn't have the time to spare to let him talk for a while. Would you? Getting in late to work would be a small price to pay for helping him. Okay, yes, I'd get some pay docked, which I could ill afford, and I'd probably get a warning, but I couldn't leave him on his own now.

Still, he didn't look into my eyes, and his frown deepened the already deep wrinkles on a face that looked like a relief map of the Himalayas. I couldn't guess at his age—eighty odd…maybe older? Was the poor chap *so* depressed he wanted to end his life now and not wait for it to end naturally?

You know, I sort of felt guilty then. Maybe I should have spent more time actually *talking* to him, finding out more about him, befriending him properly. I was busy. Work took up most of my time. The job didn't pay well and I was struggling, so I worked all the extra time I could get. I had very little time to spare for cozy chats with depressed pensioners.

Then, I remembered Gramps.

Maybe I should *make* the time. I checked my watch as surreptitiously as I could whilst taking another mouthful of food. I could just about spare an hour.

I watched as he finished his tea, then I called one of the girls over to get him a fresh one. He took it and clung to it as if it was a life saver.

"Thank you…Mike, was it?"

My mouth was full. I nodded, mopped up the last of the sauce with the end of the bread, and pushed my plate away. I needed to give him all my attention.

"So, Bill, talk to me."

He shook his head and one hand went to his chest. I wondered if he was having a heart attack, and looked around the small café. We were the only customers. There were just two girls busying themselves behind the counter. They wouldn't hear us. They had some sort of music pounding out back there. His face was really pale. Should I get an ambulance? He took a long swig of his tea, swallowed, and looked at me with a steady stare. Then, he pointed to his chest.

"This. This 'thing' has become a burden. I need to be rid of it. Maybe *you* would take…"

What on earth was he on about? I had to shake my head. There was a low buzzing noise coming from somewhere. I couldn't get rid of it. *Had* he been talking about his heart? I banged my ears with my fingers. The buzzing was still there. Must have been tinnitus.

"I don't understand, Bill. Is it your heart? Do you need a doctor?"

He smiled. He actually *smiled*, which surprised me. I don't think I'd seen him smile once in the two years I'd been meeting up with him. In his smile, I saw a younger, happier man…one without a care in the world. Then, in a flash, he was back to being the same old Bill. Only now, his hand was inside his jacket. I could see it moving about in his clothes as if searching for something. Slowly, he withdrew his hand and held it out to me, and I saw it.

The Guardian

The thing looked like it was made of solid gold. It looked heavy, too. It was attached to a long, thick, gold chain around his neck. It was one of those weird crosses with the loop on top, from Egypt or someplace—you know the sort I mean? Bill was shaking his head.

"I need no doctor; I merely need to be rid of my burden. Will you help me?"

"If I can."

"Would *you* take over my burden? Make it your own?"

He was behaving a bit weirdly, but I had to keep talking to him now. I needed to know how he'd come by such an expensive looking piece of bling. It didn't look like he had two pennies to rub together—and here he was, wearing a huge chunk of precious metal around his neck. What I wouldn't give to own a lump of bullion like that!

"I really don't think you should be flashing that thing around this place, mate. It looks a lot like gold. You never know who might see it and decide to take it from you."

The smile flashed again and his pale eyes lit up.

"It *is* indeed, solid gold. And perhaps it would be for the best if someone *should* steal it away. Then I would not have to encumber you with it."

He had a funny way of talking. I hadn't noticed before, but then, he'd hardly said anything much to me until now.

"Hey, don't say that. What can be so bad?"

I gave him a bright smile, but he wasn't looking. I let it fade.

"The mere fact I still have such a very, very long time left to exist—unless, of course, you agree to help me."

What? I noticed a strange light in his eyes, a gleam I hadn't seen before. He was getting on in years, why was he talking about having so long left? Unless he was much younger than he looked, of course. Maybe he'd just had a hard life…

"How old *are* you, Bill?"

That smile again. Today must have been a good day. I'd never seen him smile before, and now, here he was, doing it every few minutes.

"Ah, now, there's the question. How old, indeed? When I first took this burden upon myself, I was just nineteen. Long ago. So long ago…so many friends lost."

He shook his head as he looked beyond me, out of the steamy windows and into his memories.

"I'm really sorry to hear that. But if you've had it since you were nineteen, why do you want to get rid of it now, if you don't mind me asking?"

"I was told this day would come. He said I would one day wish to be rid of it, but he also said I would not be able to until someone came along who was truly willing to take it over. So far, I have not found anyone. I have asked others over the decades, they have all refused. I believe you will not."

"Well, I don't know. What are you saying? Who is 'he?' What exactly *is* your 'burden?' Why don't you tell me about it?"

He placed his cup on the table and leaned forward eagerly.

"If I told you my nineteenth birthday was in the year 1799, you would struggle to believe me, would you not?"

I did some quick mental arithmetic. Then, I did it once more, just to be sure. I'm certain my eyes were on stalks when I looked at him again. I shook my head and smiled.

"Uh—that would make you something like—two-hundred-

and-seventeen years old, Bill! I don't think so. Really. Look, let me take you back to your home. My car's just around the corner."

I was sure by now that he must live in some retirement home and his mind wasn't quite all there. Maybe he'd escaped from the wardens. He must just have got his dates mixed up. It's easy done once you get older. Gramps used to do it all the time.

"Very well, my house is not far from here, and then I shall return the favor and give you a cup of tea whilst I explain."

He left the café leaning heavily on a carved walking stick which looked even more ancient than him. He managed to get himself into my car and buckled up, giving me directions to the street where he lived. It was just two streets away from my own place.

CHAPTER TWO

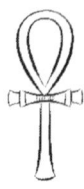

I was wrong about him living in an old folks' home. It was actually a street of mixed terraces with a row of neat bungalows. Bill pointed to one of the bungalows. I parked the car out front and followed him in. As I entered the hall behind him, we passed a large floor-to-ceiling mirror, and as we did so, our reflections almost seemed to move. I was struck with a sudden queasiness and felt a bit dizzy...must have eaten a dodgy egg.

When I pulled myself together and finally had a look around, I wasn't quite prepared for what I saw. The place looked like a museum. It was generally clean and tidy, with a squishy couch, a well-padded rocking chair, and some tasteful pieces of furniture dotted around. There were lots of large, colorful prints all over the walls—some of them by artists even I recognized.

Wherever I looked, the surfaces were covered with

artefacts, all spotless and neatly ordered, many with little white labels on them. I itched to read some of them, but reckoned it would be rude just to go diving in straight away without being asked, so I sat on the couch and shuffled a bit to get comfortable.

"Tea, with one sugar, is that right, Mike?"

He must have remembered from the times I'd sat at his table in the diner and ordered us both a second brew.

"Yes, it is, thank you."

He took off his jacket, hung it up in front of the mirror in the hall, and went into the kitchen, where I heard him puttering about. I took a chance and looked at the nearest item to me. It was a beautifully carved, dark wooden figure of a reclining Buddha, about a foot high, with such a peaceful expression on its face, I felt more relaxed almost immediately. There was a white sticker on its knee. Peering at it, I read *Buddha, hand carved, Tibet, 1850*.

Okay, well, that by itself didn't prove anything. He could have got it from an auction, or online, easy enough to do these days. I looked around as I heard the kettle come to the boil. There was a lot of military and Navy memorabilia, souvenirs from all over the world and all eras. So, he was a hoarder—a clean and tidy one—but a hoarder, nonetheless. Absently, I wondered how long it took for him to clean this lot.

Leaning heavily on his stick, Bill came back in with a cup, which he placed on the coffee table to my side of the couch, then went back out for his own drink.

"Sorry, Bill, you should have called me. I'd have come out for them. I wasn't thinking."

"Oh, it's not a problem. I need the exercise. I get stiff

sitting all day, but now that they say I'm too old to work, I don't have much choice. I spend my days cataloguing and looking after my collection."

"You do have a great collection. Where did you get them all from?"

"Oh, it would take too long today, Mike, and I am too tired now. Their labels have all the details on them. Maybe you could take a look around after you finish your tea? Each label has the date when I purchased the item and where it came from."

"Do you get them from auctions?"

He frowned, his eyes widening and lighting up with anger.

"I do not! I was present in each one of those places on those exact dates."

"So…you actually got this Buddha in Tibet, when you were—how old?"

There wasn't a second of hesitation. He hadn't needed to sit and reckon it up like I had a few moments ago. He knew immediately.

"Fifty-three. I purchased it on my birthday, August the second."

I just nodded. I'd find some way to catch him out in this silly tale.

"Funny, that's my birthday too! So, did you buy everything on birthdays?"

"Most things, yes. Each birthday served to remind me I was still alive, despite the odds."

"Despite what odds?"

"You see, I should have died on my eighteenth birthday. I did not. I felt I should celebrate the fact. Of course, as time has gone on, I don't feel quite such a need to celebrate. It is actually becoming a little stale now. Strange, I had once believed it could *never* grow stale."

"What happened to you?"

I sipped my tea and waited as he settled himself into the rocker.

"It was 1798 and I was in the Navy, on board a ship which lost many of its crew in a terrible battle. I was knocked unconscious into the sea during the conflict. I don't suppose anyone thought to look for me in the water at the time; after all, there were enough casualties on board to worry about. Most of those in the water were dead, and the fighting that day was long and fierce."

"What ship was it?"

"She was called the Majestic, carrying seventy-four guns. We were under the command of Captain George B. Westcott, serving under Rear Admiral Nelson."

I nearly spluttered my tea across the room and saw Bill looking at me with distinct amusement in his twinkling eyes. It was a joke; I knew it was. My mind simply couldn't take it in.

He could *not*—possibly—be serious!

"Nelson? *Nelson*! Do you mean Horatio Nelson? The guy who died at Trafalgar?"

"I do, indeed. Are there others?" He smiled.

"Well, damn it, I don't know. There could be. Look, I don't get this. You're *really* trying to tell me you served under Nelson at Trafalgar?"

"No! You are not listening to me, Mike. I said I served under him in the year I was eighteen. Trafalgar was some seven years after. I was in Egypt for the Battle of the Nile. We, the British of course, defeated the French at that battle, but lost a great many men. I woke up badly wounded in the water, floating on some pieces of splintered wreckage. There were bodies and body parts floating all around me, French and English. I am sorry to say...I panicked." His eyes filled with tears at the memory. "I could see land, so turned toward it and struck out. I just had to get away from the bodies, the blood, the carnage. It was my birthday. I really didn't want to spend it surrounded by my dead companions. I made land eventually, but must have passed out."

His eyes were flitting about almost as if he was seeing those terrible sights again.

"When I woke up, I was in a small tent with some elderly nomadic tribesmen. They'd seen me on the sand and rescued me. I stayed in Egypt for some time, travelling around with their tribe. I took to wearing their clothes so I would pass as one of them. I was so afraid to come back home. I knew people would say I had deserted. It was best for my family, for everyone, to believe I had been lost at sea during the battle. Deserters were not treated at all kindly in those days. I would simply have been shot without question."

He stopped talking and we sat in silence, with the ghosts of his dead comrades floating around him and that strange buzzing somewhere in the back of my head. I didn't speak. I was afraid to disturb him, and anyway, I actually wanted to hear more of this crazy, improbable tale. For some weird reason, I was becoming fascinated. I really wanted to know where he'd got the cross thing he was wearing.

Yes, I'd be late for work, but what the heck? I'd pull a sickie—everyone else did. This was better than sitting in a stuffy office any day. I shuffled on the couch, waiting for him to continue with his tale. Eventually, I had to speak, the silence around us was becoming stifling, and I was beginning to feel nauseous again.

"So, when did you come back home to England?"

"Oh, not for a long time. I had read reports of the battle in the papers. My ship had lost three officers and thirty-three seamen, they said. I don't know if that included me. Some time later, I read about the admiral's death at Trafalgar. I was sorry I couldn't have been there, too."

"When did he die?"

Again, no hesitation.

"During the battle of Trafalgar, in the year of our Lord 1805, October the twenty-first. He had been a great commander; the greatest. I was sad to hear the news."

"So, how did you get to Tibet to buy your Buddha?"

"Oh, I wandered around for many years and visited countless countries. I was young and free, and had developed a serious case of the wanderlust. I was in Tibet for my nineteenth birthday, and that was where I had the idea of starting a collection and celebrating my life by buying something each year. I did odd jobs wherever I went, enough to pay for food and transport to my next destination, and even managed to tuck away some savings. Eventually, I hired a storage area in Egypt to take all the items I was collecting along the way, and returned there often. It almost felt like my home. I would send or take my purchases to the depot and pay a little money for their safe keeping. When I finally returned to England, I shipped everything home. There were rather a lot of crates!"

He laughed. I jumped. I'd never heard him laugh before.

He was really getting into his story now, but I couldn't catch him out. I wasn't a history buff by any means, and he'd obviously had enough time to read up on all the historical facts he kept spouting. I'd be sure and check them up on the internet when I got home.

"Where did you get that necklace thing, then?"

Although I kept my voice casual, I needed to know, for some reason I had become intrigued by the pendant and wanted to know all about it.

CHAPTER THREE

"It was whilst I was on the first of my travels around Egypt after the battle. I went into a souk in Luxor to buy food, and saw an ancient man with a hunched back sitting at a corner stall. He was selling jewelry and other knick-knacks, and beckoned me in to take a look. He started pushing things at me... and asking silly prices. By then, I was fluent in the language and kept telling him I wasn't interested—until he opened his shirt, and I first saw the ankh."

"Sorry, the what?"

"The *ankh*. This."

He lifted the cross to show me again, and it gleamed in the light of his room. My head started buzzing once more. I gave it a shake.

"Oh, is that what it's called?"

I couldn't take my eyes off it. The color, the shape, the shine...I wondered how heavy it was. How it would feel around my neck? I wondered what it would be like to hold it and stroke it, like Bill did. When he spoke again, his voice jolted me back to the room.

"Yes. The merchant said it was an ancient and sacred Egyptian icon, the symbol of everlasting life and regeneration. This piece itself was, he said, thousands of years old. He asked if I was interested in it, telling me he was one-hundred-and-seventy years of age—and it was all thanks to this piece. I didn't believe him of course, any more than you believe me, now. It was simply a tall tale to entice the tourists. I did have to admit, the thing attracted me. I could not take my eyes from it as it gleamed and sparkled on his shirt. It was so beautiful. I reached out, but he pulled away and replaced it in his shirt. I asked how much he wanted. He was silent for so long I thought he had gone to sleep. Then, he said it would cost me my money *and* my life."

"Sounds like an old-fashioned highwayman to me." I smiled.

"I thought so, too. And just like you, I laughed. He was deadly serious as he explained to me what the bargain was. Oh, certainly I could have it—for a price—which, at the time, I was more than happy to pay for such a beautiful piece. The hunchback said it would bring me wealth, luck, and a very long life. There were only two conditions.

"The first, was that I take on his collection and begin adding my own. The second was, once I put on this beautiful piece, I would not be able to remove it until I found someone else willing to take it over. And…it could be a long wait. An *extremely* long wait. I knew I needed time to think about it, so I said I would meet him the next day with my answer. I did not give him his answer that day, though. Instead, I took lodgings nearby and went back to his stall many times over the following weeks. We sat together and talked a lot—much as you and I are doing now."

I couldn't help but keep looking at the piece as it lay gleaming against his shirt. I would have loved to find out how heavy it was. I wondered what it felt like around his neck; against his chest.

"Well, I guess I know what your eventual answer was, eh? It certainly is beautiful."

"Oh, indeed. It has its own individual—and quite deadly—beauty."

"Deadly? What's deadly about it?"

"Oh, when you *do* finally put it on, as well as attracting good luck and wealth to you, it has the power to rid you of your enemies. I have had people try to steal it from me on a few occasions, now. Each time, they came to a bad end without ever getting away with their booty. One, who I stood up to, turned and ran into the path of an oncoming car. Another reached out, took a firm hold of it to pull it from my neck, and suddenly seemed to have a stroke. By the time the ambulance arrived, he was dead. There have been more over the years, but as you see, I still have possession of it."

His bony hand reached up and stroked the yellow metal. It seemed to glow. I would have loved to be able to touch it. The air hummed around us. He saw me watching him, and as I looked up, his smile was wide and bright. It made him seem so much younger.

"May I take a proper look?"

As I held out my hand, it shook more than I ever

remembered it doing. Shaking his head, Bill shrank back in the chair. I drew back my hand quickly, and shuffled in my seat.

"No. You may not touch it. I will not be responsible for your fate, if you do. The only way for you to do that is to say you will take it on for life."

"Surely, it belongs in a museum if it's so ancient? Why don't you just give it to one?"

"Again, you do not listen to me. I *cannot* give it to a museum. It can only go to one individual who will agree to be its guardian for life. Of course, no museum will ever give me such a promise. Besides, it will not flourish in a museum. It has to be worn. You must see how it shines and throbs with light as I breathe?"

"I do see. But in a good show case, with lights, it would shine as brightly as it does now, surely?"

"No! There is a certain—spirit—to it, which would not thrive in the confines of a stuffy museum. It needs to be next to a beating heart to truly be alive."

Well, okay, now I reckoned he was well and truly unhinged; not dangerous, I didn't think, just crazy. It sounded as if he was saying the damn thing was actually alive. What I did know was that the strange pendant around his neck was certainly something special to look at. I found myself thinking how I could do with a bit of luck. The idea of living a long life filled with wealth certainly sounded good, even if it *was* all a fairy tale.

I looked around the room. There were a lot of interesting items here. Maybe I'd get him to tell me about them, but it would mean me coming back again. I didn't have enough time now to listen to all his tall tales. Besides, I was beginning to feel sort of—well, queer. I can't explain it any better. Just a feeling in my guts like a nest of ants was crawling around in there…and it almost felt as if there was something feeling its way up and down my back. I had to move to try and get rid of the feeling. I needed to get out of this place.

I stood up quickly.

"Look, I have to go now, but I'll give it some thought and come back to see you again. Shall we say at the weekend? You can tell me some more stories about your bits and bobs then. I'd like to hear about them."

I'd been thinking about Gramps again. If he'd been alone and depressed, I'd like to think someone would have befriended him—taken the time to let him talk and listen to him, even if he did bore them silly. Which was why I couldn't turn my back on Bill.

He looked at me with a deep frown as he clutched at the cross, and I saw him stroking it slowly. It shone so brightly, maybe his clutching fingers had rubbed a shine on it over the years he'd been wearing it. There was something within the yellow gleam…something which held my gaze and almost drew me toward it. I blinked my eyes away from its sheen as he spoke again.

"Very well. I shall look forward to telling you my 'stories' when I see you again. You know, I am well aware you believe I am just a foolish old man, but perhaps I will be able to convince you of the truth of what I say if you *do* come back. Yes, this weekend, then."

He stood up to escort me to the door, where I hesitated. I glanced down at the gleaming yellow lump hanging on his chest. I could knock him down right now and pull the thing off his neck. He couldn't stop me. He was far too frail. I shook myself in disgust. *What the hell are you thinking, Mike? Where did that come from?* I knew I couldn't really hurt him. Mad though he might be, he'd never done me any harm. Why should I be thinking about harming him? It was unlike me to think of violence like that. What on earth had come over me?

I hurried to the door, eager to be rid of those strange feelings.

"Thanks for the brew, Bill. See you at weekend then?"

"I shall look forward to it. Goodbye, for now."

At his gate, I turned and looked back. He stood on the doorstep, smiling, one hand on his stick, the other holding on to his fancy pendant. I threw him a wave and got into my car. I'd get out my computer and check out what he'd said about that sea battle when I got home, but I had a strong feeling the information he'd given me would turn out to be absolutely correct.

It was, to the letter. As I was studying it, those feelings in my guts eased up. By the time I went to bed, I was feeling fine again.

CHAPTER FOUR

The following Saturday, I knocked on Bill's door at ten-thirty. He looked pleased to see me.

"Mike. You came. Good. Come in, I'll put the kettle on."

I sat on the couch again, taking a closer look at some of the items in the room. What looked like African carvings, Chinese fans, a long and ornate Indian chief's headdress hanging on a tall coat stand in a corner, a collection of different sized boomerangs, a beat up webbing ammunition belt—hold it, were those live rounds? I'm no expert, but they looked real to me.

There were fancy sea-shells and weapons, animal's horns, even some stuffed birds and animals—the whole room seemed a bit claustrophobic. I guessed that had been what made me feel odd the last time I'd been here...all those creatures looking at me. I couldn't get my head around all the stuff in this one room, and wondered if the rest of the house contained more of his collection.

"Need some help?" I called.

"No, it's fine, just coming."

He fetched my brew in and once again went to get his. When he came back, there was a plate of biscuits balanced on the top of his mug. Carefully, he set the mug on the coffee table and took the plate from the top of it, placing it down beside my cup. He got himself settled in the rocker and looked intently at me. I felt a bit uncomfortable beneath his steady gaze, and squirmed a little. He smiled, and picked up his cup.

"Now, what was it you wanted to know?"

"Well, I'd like to know more about some of these things you have. They're interesting. That ammo belt, for instance. Are those live rounds?" I asked casually.

He smiled at me and nodded. I took a biscuit.

"They certainly are, but don't you worry, Mike. I won't shoot you for asking questions. My guns are safely under lock and key in a metal box in the bedroom."

"Guns. *Guns*—plural? How many do you have?"

Now, I was wondering if he might be a mad gunman who'd somehow find out where I lived and shoot me in my bed.

"Oh, yes, plural. I have about six—various kinds and ages, of course. But I won't take them out of their locker. I'm sorry. The ammo belt *was* mine, yes. I was in Turkey for the Crimean War. We had all been issued with new Lee-Enfields back then. I was good with mine—ten rounds a minute, I could clock up." He smiled proudly, sitting up straighter as he heard me gasp.

"Wait up! Crimean War? You meant the one with Florence

Nightingale? *Really?*"

"Really. I was shot in the shoulder. It went bad...I got a fever and ended up in one of Miss Nightingale's wards. She was a lovely lady, always ready with a kind word for the wounded. She didn't dress my wounds herself, of course, one of her nurses did. It was because of them I came through. Well, *them*, and my Egyptian souvenir, of course."

"Of course." I nodded. This was getting more than a little crazy. He smiled at me with a startling gleam in his eyes and leaned forward, as if he had a secret to tell me.

"You know, Mike, a lot of the pictures of Miss Nightingale are quite wrong."

"Wrong? In what way, wrong?" In for a penny, as they say.

"Well, they show her with the wrong sort of lamp you see, she actually used a local lamp, a Turkish folding one, not the fancy sort they have her holding in the paintings, but I suppose the local lamps weren't 'romantic' enough. They were quite plain, little more than tubes with candles inside them, but they worked well. I managed to cadge one from one of the nurses. She was quite sweet on me. It's there, on the second shelf—it's a bit fragile now, so it's behind glass. Made of something like paper, maybe skin from some small animal, with perforated copper top and bottom, and wire handle. Do you see it?"

I could see it, sitting amongst dozens of other assorted items. I made a mental note to check on that item in particular when I got my computer out later.

"Yes, I do see it. I expect you've had rather a lot of women who were 'sweet' on you over the years then, eh?"

A bright smile came to his weather-beaten face, and his

eyes twinkled as he wiggled his eyebrows at me.

"One or two, lad. One or two."

"Did you ever marry?"

"No. And I had many a long argument with myself over it. Finally, I decided it wouldn't be fair to any woman to do that to her. I didn't think I'd like it much either—me having to mourn them and still carry on with my life, after. Not fair at all. Are *you* married, Mike?"

"Nope. Never got round to it."

"Well, there's still time, if you do decide such a way is for you. You're just a youngster yet. How old are you—twenty-eight? Thirty?"

"Not far off, I'm thirty-five soon. Bit long in the tooth for marriage now, I reckon."

"Well, maybe it's a good thing."

"Good, how?"

"Well, you see, if you do decide to take my burden on, you would have to make the same decisions I made about lovers. And believe me, it has to be better not to get too deeply involved. Love 'em and leave 'em, son—it's for the best. No regrets that way. What else would you like to know about?"

The gold gleamed brightly on his chest, moving gently as he breathed, its shine lifting, then darkening almost as if it was breathing, also. I had to gaze at it. There were such a lot of things I wanted to know. Where to begin?

I drew my reluctant gaze away from the gleaming symbol and looked around the room. The painting above the fire drew my eye straight away. A bright, colorful, almost abstract design of tall, blue flowers, with smaller yellow-colored ones in the background, and a single, taller white one almost in the center,

The Guardian

I was sure I'd seen something similar somewhere before.

"That painting—what's its story?" I pointed.

He nodded slowly and looked at the painting with what seemed to me like a deep sadness.

"Ah, that one. I believe I treasure it almost above all of my collection. The artist was a dear friend."

"*Was?* When did he die?"

"July, 1890, not long before my birthday. It was a sad time. His mind was disturbed. Poor Vincent committed suicide. Shot himself. Such a terrible loss to the art world."

I looked at the picture again, now I recognized the style. He had to be joking. Surely not.

"*Vincent?* As in Van Gogh?"

"The same. It was shortly before my one-hundred-and-eleventh birthday. Of course, I still looked much younger then, so I was able to mix with him and his artist friends in Paris, including Paul Gauguin. It was because of Gauguin that Vincent damaged his ear, you know?"

My mind was just about refusing to take in any more of this stuff, but I decided to go along with it for a while longer. I had nothing better to do, and anyway, it was keeping me entertained.

"No, I didn't know. Tell me about it?"

"Well, I wasn't actually there, of course."

"Of course." *No, you were probably sitting in your living room reading a book about them.*

"I was in the next village when the news reached there. It was 1888, around Christmas time. Vincent and Gauguin had a terrible fight, Vincent grabbed up a cut-throat razor and threatened to kill Paul with it. They eventually made up, but poor Vincent's mind was troubled, had been for some time. He felt so guilty for threatening to kill Gauguin, he slashed off his own ear in his despair. He was a genius…and as we know, genius and madness are separated by only the finest of lines."

"And where did the painting come from? Or is it a print?"

"Go and take a closer look. You will see it most certainly is not a print. Vincent gave it to me himself. After he had cut off his ear, he took himself away to an asylum in Saint-Remy—and, in one way, I believe it did him good. He created so many fine paintings there. I went to visit a few times, and on my last visit, he presented me with this. I treasure it. There were two later versions I believe, one of which his brother, Theo, submitted to an exhibition, where it was sold to a world famous art critic. I think the other, a smaller one, is now in a museum in Canada."

"Well, if that really is by Van Gogh, it must be worth a small fortune; maybe even a huge fortune. Why not sell it and live off the earnings?"

"Never! I will never part with any of my artefacts. These things are all a part of me, of my long life. They *are* my life. They are the signposts to every significant thing which has ever happened to me. When it is time for me to go, I shall be passing my collection over to the person who takes on my burden, as the old man in the souk did with me. That person will not be able to sell anything. He will not physically be able to part with any item, no matter how insignificant it may look. The treasures all have to stay together. They are all—connected. There is no way they can be separated."

Suddenly, he looked stronger and fitter than I'd ever seen him. I was almost concerned he might attack me, he seemed so agitated as he rocked to and fro, balancing right on the front edge of his chair and clutching the necklace as if his life depended on it. I needed to try and calm him down a bit before he did rush me.

"Bill, take it easy, mate, I'm not going to take anything from you. Don't worry. Calm down before you have a heart attack or something." *And if you did, it'd damn well teach me not to go befriending weird old men wearing bling.*

Gradually, he relaxed back into his chair, still holding onto the Egyptian cross. I watched as his face eased itself back into the same soft features it had worn before. Maybe I should leave now, and not come back... I really didn't want to be responsible for the old fellow shuffling off whilst I was anywhere around. How could I explain that? And what would happen to the necklace? I couldn't let anyone else have it now, could I? It was mine.

Apparently, we just had a simple bargain to make, then as soon as it was on my neck, he could pop his clogs whenever he was ready. *Damn it. Mike, have you any idea how callous you sound? Surely, you're not so desperate for a bit of tat to sling round your neck?* I shivered.

'Cold, are you, Mike? I can put the heating on for a while if you wish? I enjoy all these mod cons we have now. Nothing like them when I was a lad, of course."

"No, no, I'm not cold. I'm fine, thanks. Just someone walking over my grave is all."

He just nodded and smiled, like he knew exactly what I meant, and in that moment, I swear he could read my mind! I certainly hoped not. It hadn't actually been *me* thinking those things. I'm not like that. Really, I'm not. But I expect everyone will say the same thing when there's a huge chunk of precious metal at stake.

I didn't like the way my mind seemed to be working by itself all of a sudden, nor did I like the way my stomach was twisting around inside me like a snake. Once again, I was beginning to feel sick, and I excused myself, saying I would be back the following day. I couldn't wait to get out of the place. Suddenly, it had started pressing in around me and giving me the willies something rotten. I practically ran to my car to get away.

I would check out his latest odd stories, and tomorrow I'd go back and take a closer look at some of the items in his home...maybe try and catch the old fellow out in his tall tales.

I'd been going to his house for a few weeks, mostly at weekends, listening to his tales, and checking them out on my computer. So far, I hadn't been able to find fault with any of his stories. Could it *really* be possible? Could he really be as old as he said he was?

It seemed impossible, but there was a ring of truth to his words I couldn't afford to ignore if I wanted the gold.

CHAPTER FIVE

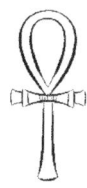

One Sunday lunch time, I was back at his door, itching to go in and find out more. There was no answer to my knock, so I pressed the bell and left my finger on it for a while. Still nothing. My heart began to beat faster. What if he had collapsed? What if he was lying on the floor in there—dead? Who'd get the ankh then? The paramedics? The police? *It should be me.*

But what if he'd done a moonlight flit? What if he'd packed up and gone someplace else because I couldn't make up my mind about his stories. *No! He wouldn't have gone so quickly; he couldn't move everything so fast. Besides, why would he leave, now that he's hooked me into his world and got me lusting after his lump of metal?*

I went to each of his windows in turn and peered in. Each room was still filled with his collection, but empty of his body—thank goodness. So maybe he'd just gone for a walk. It was a nice late summer day, after all. Suppose he'd gone out and been attacked? Had the thing stolen? What would I do then?

As I stood by his front door wondering whether to call the police, I heard a noise behind me. My knees turned to jelly when I saw him hobbling up the path with a carrier bag and a big smile. He was okay! Thank goodness.

"Hello, Mike. Been waiting long?"

"Where have you been?" I think I was a little sharper with him than I should have been.

"Went to the local shop to get us a bit of cake to have with our tea."

He lifted the bag to show me as he walked past and opened his front door. I followed him in and closed the door behind us while he took off his coat and went into the kitchen. I headed for the living room again and wandered around, looking at the labels on the artefacts.

The feeling of not being alone in the room filled my soul. I knew Bill was out in the kitchen. I could hear him getting out the cups. I looked around, positive there was someone else in there with me.

"You want to come and get the cups, Mike? I'll bring the cake."

"Sure, I'm on my way." Anything to escape from that odd feeling.

The small but tidy kitchen was also filled with objects. I had a quick glance around, then picked up the cups and carried them back into the living room. Bill followed with a plate full of cake slices. We sat in our favorite places, neither saying a word, both looking into the steam from our brews as we formulated our own thoughts.

The Guardian

"So, Mike?"

The sudden sound of his voice was loud in the silence of the crowded room, and made me jump.

"Yes. Yes, what?"

"Have you had enough time now to come to a decision?"

"There are still some things I need to know first."

"I guessed there would be. Fire away."

"Well, if I do take this—burden—on, what will *you* do? Stay here? Move to a home? What?"

"If you do take on the ankh, I shall simply disappear. My time has come. I believe it had come long ago, but there was no one around then to relieve me. Until I can let it go, I am not able to end my journey here."

"So, you—go, and where do all your things end up?"

"You take them on and begin adding your own artefacts to them, of course. As I did, when I took it on from the man in the market."

"And your house—you said you have no family. I assume you actually own this place, so who will get it when you do—*go*?" I shrugged, embarrassed to use the word for some reason. Bill however, had no such problem with it and looked me straight in the eye with an unsettling pale blue stare.

"When I do *die*, it will all belong to you. Don't worry, the provisions have all been made, and no questions will be asked. You will simply take over from me. You can then either move in and stay here, or sell this house and move to a place more suited to you. Along with the collection, of course. The choice is yours."

"But I know nothing about any of these things."

I looked around us at the collection. He laughed, a hollow,

echoing sound in the crowded room. That had me feeling a bit creeped out, I don't mind telling you.

"Oh, you will have a long time to find out. In the cabinet beside the front door, there is a shelf filled with my notebooks. I have kept them since I first landed on Egypt's shores. They tell of my travels, all my purchases, my friends. Everything you might need to know is within those pages. I write a little each day, so they are up-to-date. They will make for extremely interesting reading, I am sure. And you can begin making your own notes for when the time comes that you wish to pass on your burden to another."

I had seen the notebooks, of course, and longed to take a look at them.

"But I don't know if I want to do it. How has it worked out for you? It sounds to me as if you'd rather have not taken it on back then."

Well, okay, so I was beginning to believe the stories. Far-fetched though they were, I hadn't been able to fault anything he'd said so far.

"You need more time? Take it. Take as long as you like, but remember, I am tired. Recently, I have been actively looking for *someone* to take my burden from me as soon as possible. My time has come. I was merely waiting for the right person to come along. And here you are. Think about it. All the money and luck you could ever want will be yours, simply for the asking—all the while you hold on to the ankh. You will age of course, but very, very slowly. I will admit, there have been times when I have wished I had never met the hunchback, but they have been few compared to the enjoyment and luck the cross has brought to me down the years."

He took a hold of the gleaming pendant and rubbed his fingers over it. A sound like the song of a thousand bees filled the room and swirled inside my head for a couple of seconds, then faded. The gold shot arrows of brilliant light around the room, flashing onto the full cupboards and collection of pictures on the walls.

I wanted to touch the thing so much my mouth was almost watering.

"But there is still such a lot I need to know. I can't just take this on without knowing more about it."

"I have more than enough time left to tell you anything you wish. But can *you* spare the time to sit with me and let me ramble on about times and centuries gone by?"

"I don't wish to sound rude, but I think I need to see more proof. Everything you've told me up to now could have been taken from reference books. Is there anything you can show me which will give me irrefutable proof?"

I had already seen there weren't enough books in the house for him to have gained all the information he'd been giving to me, and I don't think he had a computer.

"Photographic evidence, you mean?" he smiled.

"Well, that might work, yes. Do you actually have photographs with you in them? I mean, photography hadn't been invented in Nelson's day, had it?"

"No, not quite in Nelson's day. It came along some few years later. But, of course, I have always tried to avoid being anywhere near a camera. There could be some awkward questions, otherwise. I do have one or two snapshots of groups of people in different parts of the world, where I have accidentally been a part of the group. However, if you are looking for pictures of me with famous historical figures, I am afraid you will be disappointed, my friend. My word will have to be my bond."

Okay, so I was no wiser as to the truth of what he was saying. But really...I think I was actually starting to believe him. I hadn't found fault with any of his details, but I'm a naturally suspicious person. Always have been. I ate my piece of cake slowly, all the time thinking over everything I'd learned about this strange man in these last few weeks.

Suddenly, I felt a squirming in my belly and down my back again. I looked up. Bill had hold of the ankh and was rubbing it gently with one gnarled hand as he sipped at his tea.

Once more, I felt a pressure around me. I heard the low song of bees, as bright slivers of golden light flashed and danced around the crowded room. I *had* to have the thing, no matter what.

I put down my cup and looked at Bill. He was smiling, gripping the cross with two hands now, and looking at me with a strange expression on his face. Suddenly, I recognized it. *Sadness. But for whom? Me? Or him?* I made up my mind.

"Very well. I will take on your burden."

He relaxed and leaned back in his chair, with a sigh so deep it must have come from his boots.

"You do not know how pleased I am with your decision, Mike. Do you have to give notice at work? Sort out any affairs? Pay any bills? Talk to your family? All of those will need to be put straight, first. You cannot afford for anyone to come looking for you. These days, it is far harder to hide in plain sight, which is why I am so tired, I think...from constantly having to cover my tracks. I hope you will find it easier to get someone to take over when your time finally comes."

"I only have to give a week's notice at work. I have no outstanding bills or any other 'affairs' to sort out, and no family to tell. By next weekend, I can be as free as a bird."

"And what about your house and furniture? Remember, you will have to come and live here. My collection cannot be without a curator."

"I live in a rented, pokey, one bed apartment. What furniture is mine is not worth anything, and my personal belongings can go into a couple of suitcases. I can be here by next Sunday with my bags packed. But where will you go?"

"Leave it to me. Just be here by noon next Sunday, with all you will need."

As I left, I felt the sickness I'd come to expect from this place churning in my stomach. It always seemed worse as I was leaving—almost as if it was trying to get me to stay... *Stupid idiot. Where'd you get such a barmy idea from?*

Those bees were singing again as I left. Bill closed the door softly behind me.

I needed to get to the silence of my own home and toss this decision over in my head. It was right, I knew it was. This would mean I'd have the necklace, as well as all the artefacts in the house, to do with exactly as I wished.

I reckoned I'd sell the whole lot as soon as possible. I could use the money to travel, like Bill had done. Or to buy a really good house somewhere away from here.

CHAPTER SIX

The following Sunday was August the second, my birthday, and here I was—about to start a new life. I locked my front door for the last time and pushed the key through the letter box. I'd spent the week working out my notice and sorting what the old fellow liked to call my "affairs."

It was all done and dusted, my bags were packed and here I was, standing on the doorstep of the place where I'd lived for the last ten years, ready to move into a strange, crowded place with—well, who knew *how* many precious things just lying about for the taking.

I have to admit to having a few minutes of hesitation. Damn it, I'd invested a heck of a lot of time getting to know Bill Crowley. If I backed down now, I'd have nothing. Nothing at all—no job, no friends, no car, nowhere to live… I had no choice any more.

I headed for his place with my two fat suitcases trailing

along behind me like anchors.

He opened the door to my knock with a big smile on his old face. Well, I say old, but today, he looked much younger than I'd ever seen him. It even almost looked as if the wrinkles were disappearing. He certainly seemed stronger, and he was no longer using a stick as he had when I had first met him.

"Come in, my friend. Come in and take the weight off."

I left my cases in his hall and parked on the couch. I didn't know what to do now. I was drifting in a dream with nothing...no one...no place. If Bill changed his mind now, I'd be stuffed. I was in a void, and it was filled with the strange bee song and flashing golden lights.

"So, what do we do now?" My voice didn't belong to me.

"You need do nothing, just sit there. I will do all that is needed."

He caressed the ankh and the bee song soared in the space around me as my stomach twisted and churned and my back crawled with snakes of ice. The room grew darker, and suddenly, I was afraid. I wanted to change my mind. I wanted to run. I couldn't move my legs. My body was so heavy I couldn't even do my shuffle to rid it of the terrible feelings which were closing in around me, filling my body and brain.

Bill sat beside me on the couch, the first time he'd ever sat so close. I was surprised. More so when he reached out and took my hand. I couldn't draw it away from his surprisingly tight grip. I couldn't even make the effort to pull it away from him. He smiled as he lifted it to the cross. At last, I was going to get to touch it, which was all I'd wanted for so long—just to hold the beautiful pendant, just to feel its weight and smoothness.

Oh, and it *was* smooth. Years of stroking had smoothed its surface, polishing it to a dazzling shine. As he placed my fingers on it, I was surprised to feel it was icy cold—not warm, as I had somehow expected it to be.

"Take hold of it, Mike. Wrap your fingers around it and close your eyes. When you open them again, it will all be done."

I could hear his breathing, and feel the heat of his body pressed against my side.

I took a deep breath and did as he asked.

Everything began to spin around me. The stuffed animals came alive and swirled around, calling and crying, squeaking and chirping. The bees sang loudly, and searing yellow flashes dived into my brain like lightning bolts.

Suddenly, there was a huge explosion…then another. To my addled brain, it sounded like cannon fire. My mind started playing a horrific film of a huge black sea, frothing with blood and body parts as the sounds of a violent battle rang out all around me.

The noise was more than deafening. The light was more than dazzling.

I couldn't close my eyes tightly enough to escape its brilliance—or those terrible sights. The air was being sucked from the room, and from my lungs. I was drowning. I began gasping for breath. Still, I was unable to move to help myself as the whole room pressed in and swirled around me. Lights flashed as cannons roared.

A blessed darkness gradually descended over the room and the sounds died away. I became aware of my body still sitting upright on the couch, as I had previously been. The nausea returned as the sounds diminished. Then, the cold began. A bone deep, soul deep cold…the likes of which I had never before experienced.

As the feeling returned to my body, I began shivering. Slowly, the warmth returned to me and I was aware of a weight around my neck, pressing heavily on my chest. A huge silence surrounded me. I sat there for…I have no idea for how long…afraid to open my eyes, afraid of what I was going to see when I did. Afraid of what my future would now be.

I listened for Bill's breathing. The silence hurt my ears, and flooded my brain. I became aware he was no longer sitting beside me. I also realized I was now stroking the golden cross. It felt large and smooth; warm, and strangely comforting somehow.

With a gulp, I cracked a gap in my eyes. It was daylight—not dark, as I had expected it would be. Opening my eyes properly, I looked around. It was the same room, the same couch. Looking down, I saw my hand, like a claw, clutching the pendant close to my chest. Bill was nowhere to be seen.

Gradually, I felt able to stand up and look around the rest of the house for any sign of him. I entered his bedroom, and there, on the pillow, was a brown envelope with my name on it. I opened it with shaking fingers, sitting on the bed as I read what was on the single sheet of paper.

Mike. I wish you luck for the rest of your long life. You are now the Guardian of my treasures. You will know when the time comes for you to begin looking for someone to take over. Do not worry about me. I am in a place of peace—a place to which I should have gone many years ago. Thank you. Happy Birthday, Mike. Yours. Bill Crowley.

I heard a sound at the front door and stood up to go and

see what it was. A letter lay on the mat. I opened the door to see the postman at the gate. He turned when he heard the door open.

"Nice day, Mr. Crowley."

He waved and walked away. Puzzled, I picked up the letter and shut the door.

As I passed the large hall mirror, I looked into it.

Bill Crowley was looking back at me!

Younger, with less wrinkles, darker hair, and only a slightly hunched back, but definitely, with no doubts whatsoever—it *was* Bill.

I dropped the letter.

The reflection smiled.

I grabbed the ankh, and the bee song soared around me.

ABOUT THE AUTHOR

Gil McDonald is an English author, who also writes Western Romance for Prairie Rose Publications, and traditional Westerns for Robert Hale in London.

A widow, Gil lives in the North of England, close to her married daughter and two grandchildren, and not far from her mother and two sisters. She shares her home with a pair of Miniature Schnauzer 'girls,' who like to try and help with the writing.

Although she has been writing for many years, and has seven publications to her name, on both sides of the 'Pond,' 'The Guardian,' is the first supernatural story she has ever submitted, anywhere. She is thrilled that Fire Star Press has taken her on. Now she might have a go at writing some more!

To find out more about Gil, go to her website – www.womanwholeads.webs.com.

EYES LIKE THE SEA

When Lucas Brody stops by a small farm to ask for water for his horse, a beautiful young woman greets him with a pistol in hand. Martha Thompson soon realizes she's made a mistake—she needs this drifter's help desperately. Exhausted, alone, and afraid, Martha collapses and must rely on this stranger for her very life. But can she trust him? Someone is trying to steal her land. Luke vows to discover who is tearing down her fences—and manages to put himself directly in harm's way. Bushwhacked, tortured, and left for dead by the ruthless gang of outlaws, he struggles back to the farm—only to find it has been burned down. Time is short, and Luke has a decision to make. He'll do anything to protect Martha, the woman he's come to love...the woman with EYES LIKE THE SEA...

HEARTS and RED RIBBONS

When a beautiful horse charges into their yard one spring evening, Mrs. Jones and her tomboy daughter, Marlee, can't know how much their lives will change. Marlee goes in search of the owner of the big horse, only to be jumped by an injured man. He's hurt badly, and Marlee must get him home to safety.

Ben Chambers is searching for something, but until he meets Marlee Jones, he doesn't know what. Settling down is the last thing Ben wants, but he can't seem to convince himself of that around Marlee. Valentine's Day is upon them and there's only one thing to do—tie Marlee's heart to his own with a special red ribbon, and let the courtship begin!

SAINT or SINNER

Leroy Vance is a hard hearted bounty hunter, hot on the heels of a gang of outlaws, when he gets his horse shot out from under him. Injured, and on foot, in the wide flat lands, Vance faces almost certain death. Help comes in the form of a buggy driven by two foreigners, father and son. They take him to the nearest town, and drive off without a word. When he eventually tries to buy a new horse, Vance is directed to the ranch owned by the foreigners. There, he finds some excellent stock. But the ranch holds a secret. The foreigners don't train the horses themselves; that is done by the wife of the younger man, and her little brother, who are both abused and beaten by the men. Vance swears to rescue the woman and boy. But Fate has a few tricks up her sleeve, and a lot can change in a short time. Vance falls in love with the man's wife as he helps them to escape. But with her husband hot on their heels, will the trio escape? And will Leroy Vance, bounty hunter and sinner, finally find True Love with the wife of another man?

Made in the USA
Charleston, SC
11 October 2016